HOWL

A SHORT FANTASY STORY

SUPER GREAT CHALLENGE STORIES
BOOK TEN

RYAN M. WILLIAMS

Glittering Throng Press

PO BOX 179

RAINIER WA 98576-0179

eBook ISBN-13: 978-1-946440-96-9

Paperback ISBN-13: 978-1-946440-97-6

GTP NO. 52
SGC NO. 10

Acknowledgments

This story is one of 52 weekly stories written (and published) over a year. It's part of the Super Great Challenge (SGC) run by Dean Wesley Smith and Kristine Kathryn Rusch through the WMG Publishing workshops on Teachable. Without that challenge, this story (and the others) likely wouldn't exist.

Additionally, in creating the cover art for the stories in the SGC, I've typically used Blender—my **favorite application ever**—an open source, free, 3D modeling, digital painting, animation, sculpting, and video editing application. I've taken courses and watched tutorials from creators like Ducky 3D, SouthernShotty, Grant Abbitt, Curtis Holt, Ryan King, the Blender Studio, CG Cookie, CG Boost, the Blender Guru and so many others. It's a wonderful and inspiring community.

And I'm so grateful for the **support**

of my members on my site (ryan mwilliams.com) for their encouragement for this challenge. My family has also been instrumental in making this possible. It helps immensely having people behind me on this journey. Thank you.

CHAPTER I
HOWL

Cold October air frosted the branches and eaves. It nurtured delicate ice crystals across the fallen dry leaves so they crunched like maple candy with each step. Woodsmoke flavored the breeze, weak trickles crawling out of the chimneys, exhausted after burning all night to keep the freeze at bay. Pin pricks (*faerie ice picks*) lanced through Howl's blue jeans, biting into his skinny legs as he walked. The fabric was stiff and rough against his skin. It did little to keep in any warmth. His purple coat puffed out around his arms, leaving his wrists exposed, and barely reached the top of his thighs. The front didn't close

—he had tied it up with shoe laces strung through holes punched in the fabric. Beneath it he wore two flannel shirts over a fraying undershirt stained with his sweat. His bright orange beanie was pulled down over his long gray hair. He hunched shoulders against the straps of his backpack and kept his head down, watching the frosted sidewalk, his taped shoes crushing the frosty leaves.

Too cold to sleep last night. Good way to freeze. Fog puffed out from his nose, forming ice crystals on his thick gray mustache and beard. *Keep moving. Get to the mall. That back retaining wall faced south, mostly. Sun'll warm it. Can get a cup of hot chocolate and a cup of hot water from Nan's on the way. Enough for his instant oatmeal.*

But damn, its cold.

Empty streets. No one out in this cold.

Fifty-six years old, Howl figured, last summer. Not how he'd thought it'd go, two years ago. It might as well been a decade ago. His joints complained. No pain killers. Used to take that for granted. Got an ache, take something. Easy peasey, easy come, easy go. 'Cept it'd never been easy.

He lifted his head, squinting against the bright sun and the sparkling trees. Wincing against the air freezing his throat, he let out a long, "Aroooo!"

A crow in one of the trees hopped from one branch to another and scolded him.

Howl sucked more razor-sharp air and let out a louder, longer, cry into the morning air. "Ar ar aroooo!"

An answering call came from a yard hidden behind a tall plastic fence. Deep-throated, a dog responding, "Aroooo-arrroooo!"

"Arr, arr, arroooooo, ar aroooo," Howl sang into the early morning.

He adjusted the straps on his backpack and went on, mouth closed, throat stinging, but he grinned as the dog returned one more mournful call.

CHAPTER 2
NAN'S

Nan's Drive-thru was shuttered and closed, plywood up over the windows. Howl stopped, legs braced, and studied the stand. *Closed? It looked permanently closed. Boarded up.* He licked cracked lips, tongue tasting the icy air like licking a razor blade.

When had he last been over here? Last week, wasn't it? Had to be. Or late the previous week. Maybe.

It was boarded up good. Sheets nailed in place to cover the windows. Thick shiny padlock attached to the the door. Chalk board that had the specials hastily rubbed out, and a chalk scrawled message.

"Out of Business. Thank the A.I."

Howl shuffled around, hooded eyes scanning the mall parking lot. Only cars in the outskirts, windows covered and fogged. Some with flat tires. Still some sort of shelter. Only cars in the lot right now. *Had the mall closed?* He couldn't remember. It might have. Might have.

He half-turned, looking back at Nan's. She'd been a tough gal. Older, even than him, he thought. Gaunt-looking, with this gray hair pulled back tight. Didn't like talking about herself. Took up the stand when Social Security shut down. Guess it didn't work out.

Shit fuckers.

His legs had gone numb, but standing there, the sun brought back the stabbing pains. He took one shuffling step. Another. One foot in front of the other, right. The retaining wall looked a long way away, but unoccupied. Might catch some warmth from the sun and a couple hours sleep. He shuffled on, remembering.

CHAPTER 3

BEFORE

It never made sense to Carter Horton, and he was an IT guy. People didn't understand what he did most of the time. That was fine. It came down to helping people, bottom-line. Complex systems that needed someone to look after it, make sure things ran as they should. Did the maintenance that any machine needed. Now, though, people thought they could ask an A.I. and get back a correct answer—no matter how many times it was shown that the answers were often biased or incorrect. He put down his phone on the kitchen breakfast table and rubbed his eyes.

Nate sat across the table, his lean

(*hollowed*) face lifted from his own phone. "Everything okay?"

Carter picked up his orange juice and took a sip. "All this A.I. crap. Who do they think is going to buy anything, if people are out of work?"

"I thought new technology always ended up creating more jobs?"

Carter shook his head. "If that was true, its hardly efficient, is it? Technology is usually a way to redistribute wealth from the poor to the wealthy."

"Isn't your entire thing passed on tech?"

"Yes, but they're talking about signing up with this automated sys admin thing our vendor is offering."

Now Nate sat up straighter. "You're serious? What does that mean for your job?"

"If they go through with it? I'll probably be out of work."

"That's, hon, that's terrible. We can't afford everything on only my salary. What about Kathy's school tuition? And there's that France trip, you know she has her heart set on it."

"I know. But the vendor claims that

between their A.I., and their support system, they can take over the sys admin functions for less. When I argue against it I know they just think that I'm being self-serving. The vendor sells that with their sys admin package, it works 24/7, never needs a day off. Is always available. And anyone can submit a ticket to the A.I. to address any problems—that it can handle everything in parallel."

"That sounds pretty great, actually," Nate said, chuckling.

"Gee, thanks."

"No, no. You know I think they're crazy. I get their pitch, that's all. We have some people in the lab that I could probably replace with the A.I. package our reps keep pushing. Except with our work, it could mean life and death. It raises the bar."

"I thought I'd reach retirement, at least, before they did anything like this. Ten years, that's all I wanted. Instead they're talking about it now. And Congress has that social security vote coming up."

Nate pushed aside his plate and put

down his phone. His large brown eyes looked wide, frightened. "You're really serious? This could actually happen?"

"Yes!" Carter pushed back his chair and stood up. "That's what I'm trying to tell you. They could eliminate my position. Congress could end social security. Even if I wanted to retire early —I'm too young. But I don't think my chances of going into a similar job are very high either."

Nate stood also and moved around the table. He reached out and pulled Carter into a hug, holding him close, as he stroked Carter's hair.

"We'll work it out," Nate said.

CHAPTER 4

RETAINING WALL

It hadn't worked out.

Howl pulled his thoughts away from all of that. *How much was real?* He didn't know anymore. Thinking about those memories, where they even real? Had he been that person? He *remembered* it, but it seemed like something. that might have happened to someone else, like in a movie or something. *Except when had he seen a movie?* Couldn't remember that either.

The morning sun was burning off some of the cold on the back of his legs as he shuffled to the retaining wall. Not exactly warm, but it didn't feel like he was getting a tattoo from a ice-pick wielding fairies now. Not on the back of his legs.

It was a mixed blessing. Even the hint of a thaw roused muscle aches from their hibernation. Pains shot up his right leg from behind his knee. He limped as the knee threatened to lock up.

He lifted his head slightly, looking for the retaining wall. *Not far now.* Closer than expected.

He stumbled to a stop.

It wasn't unoccupied.

There'd been no one the last time he looked this way, he was sure of it. Now, though, there were several figures all around the base of the retaining wall, and tents. Dogs and children ran around the tents and it was the tents that drew his attention.

Each tent stood alone on the the cracked asphalt in front of the retaining wall. *Weird.* The tents were rectangular and long, with peaked brown tops that rose to a point at each end and then sagged slightly in the middle. They looked like roofs, more than a tent, and the tent fabrics beneath were brightly colored. One had vibrant sunflower-yellow walls. Another was done an a deep jade green. The one with blue walls was a soft cerulean shade. He counted seven of the tents arranged in two rows from the retaining wall outward, except the distance between increased with each tent so they formed a 'V' shape. The tent at the point, right back up against the retaining wall, was the largest. The lower fabric on that one was a dark grape purple decorated in shining gold stars and swirls. The collection could have been a carnival of sorts—except the tents were all *small*. Howl couldn't judge easily, but the roof on the largest didn't rise above the retaining wall.

He scratched his chin through the rough beard, considering.

They hadn't been there, had they?

Howl couldn't be sure. The freezing cold and lack of sleep, plus the perpetual ache in his belly, made thinking back a challenge. *Had he seen it was unoccupied?* Or had he *wanted* it to be unoccupied? Like planning to get coffee and hot water for his oatmeal at Nan's. Except Nan's was closed. Out of business.

He shuffled around and looked back at the drive thru.

Still boarded up.

"Woof," he said softly. Hadn't imagined that, had he?

Except he had thought it'd be open. He'd known Nan closed up. He remembered her thin face, the lines around her eyes, telling him something about closing up. She was gonna move, go to one of the camps down in Nevada? Wyoming? Some place like that.

"I couldn't do that," he had said.

She said something, then said, "Institutional, sure, but it's a roof and meals every day. Beats staying in my car—which doesn't run now, even if I still had a license."

Howl closed his eyes, taking a deep breath.

"Man, don't," Nan said.

He threw back his head and howled, a long, mournful warble into the sky. When the last echoes faded, he'd looked down at his steaming cup of coffee. He sipped it. Turned away from the drive thru, and walked away.

"You're crazy, Howl. Take care of yourself," Nan said.

He thought she said that. It was something like that. Unless she didn't.

Earlier he hadn't remembered any of that, begging the question if it was a real memory or not? Didn't seem to matter much either way. Nan's was closed. She probably was off in some institutional "camp." *Prison.* State housing for the unemployed masses. Put to work for the privilege. Some, like Nan, figured it better than living out here.

Thank the A.I. It made it all possible.

Howl looked back toward the retaining wall, thinking of the warmth there from the sun. The tents, the 'V' formation meant none of them cast shadows on the others. And they took up the whole space in front of the retaining wall.

Three children, small bodies running swiftly, chased after a long-legged, scruffy, black and white dog. It easily out-distanced them, dodging and yapping as it raced away around a tent. Laughing in high voices, the children chased after, hands going up to hold their long, pointed hats on their heads. They also disappeared around the tent.

Long, pointed hats? Howl starred, watching for the children to reappear. They'd been wearing pointed hats. One a bright yellow, one cherry red, and the last in a sky blue color. It had to be a new trend, something the kids were doing, but he hadn't seen it anywhere else.

They exploded back into view from the other side of the tent, darting into the center space between the tents. Other children were about too he saw, larger than the three chasing the dog, watching with amused faces beneath pointed hats. He saw a couple reach up, stroking beards that hung down over their bellies.

Howl lifted a hand covered in a

glove and mitten, rubbing the cold knit across his face.

What he saw hadn't changed much. Except the dog was racing across the parking lot straight at him, with the children still in pursuit.

CHAPTER 5

CHILDREN

Bright sunlight shone upon the charging dog and the children pursuing it. Their breaths were like puffs of smoke from an old train stack, *puff, puff, puff* as the ran. The dog looked back over its shoulder, tongue wagging unconcernedly in the frosty air, then its head turned back an it saw Howl standing in its path only a couple dozen feet away. Dark eyes (*one surrounded by black fur, the other by white fur*) widened with surprised.

Howl threw back his head and said, "Ar ar arrooooo!"

As he looked down, the dog skidded to a stop. It planted its legs wide and panted, staring at him. Not scared or nervous, but curious. Howl grinned and tried again.

"Ar arr arroooo!" The warbling cry rose with his fogging breath.

The dog sat down, black-tipped tail sweeping back and forth across the asphalt. The three children came to a stop behind the dog in a semi-circle, watching Howl.

He winked, smiled, and then lifted his head again. "Ar ar arroooo arooo!"

Before he finished, the dog threw back its head and joined him, howling, "Arroooo rooo."

The children laughed and clapped. Lowering his head again, Howl crouched down and held out a hand toward the dog. It rose and trotted easily over to him, grinning a doggy grin as it sniffed at his mittened and gloved hand. Then it moved in closer, pressing up against his palm, turning to give him better access to rub its back.

"Good boy," Howl said. "You're a good boy, aren't you?"

"Girul!" One of the children said,

giggling, her voice accented. "She's a girul!"

"Okay," Howl said. "Good girl, then. You're a good girl."

He scratched and the dog shook herself back and forth beneath his hand. He stroked her scruffy fur, marveling how her black and white coloration continued from her head down to her tail. Not entirely even, the dividing line looped and curled, with spots of black and white on the opposite sides, but she was *mostly* white on her left side, and *mostly* black on her right side.

"What is her na..." Howl broke off his question and he looked up at the children crowding closer and got his first really good look at them.

Three wizened faces peered at him with large eyes surrounded by wrinkles of skin. All of them had beards of white and gray that hung down their front and ended in short braided ends. Their eyes ranged from blue to a stormy gray, hues of skin tone from a light brown tan to a pale pink, almost white. He'd already seen their pointed hats, but they also wore thick felted vests that matched their hat colors and material. Beneath the vests, they had white long-sleeve shirts, dark blue denim pants, and solid leather boots. Laces everywhere, on the boots, their pants, the shirt, and the vest —all made from leather as well. They wore their hair long, touching their shoulders, and it was as white and gray as their beards. And they had pointy ears that peeked out of their long curly hair.

The one in the red hat spoke in a high, girlish voice. "What's your name?"

All of them were looking at him, interested, waiting. Even the dog. He coughed. His knees ached, so he straightened up, pressing his mittens together.

"Uh, I'm called Howl."

All three kids (*not kids, unless...costumes?*) giggled with bright cheer. The one who had asked his name pointed to (*her*) chest and said, "I'm Nutmeg. They're Lodge, short for Lodgepole, and Acorn. Is H'owl really your name?"

Nutmeg's features, despite their

apparent age (*and the beard*) looked like those of girl. They all seemed like they were seven or eight years old (*except for looking like seventy or eighty years old.*) She smiled brightly at him. The dog, seeing that no one was offering imme-diate attention, wandered around, sniffing the asphalt.

"Um, it's what people call me. Ah, nickname? Its who I am now."

She nodded and suddenly they all had solemn, serious expressions. He couldn't place her accent, but it was charming. "But nut who you've always been, correct?"

He nodded.

"What did people call you before?"

Howl opened his mouth and nothing came out. He frowned. He knew his name, of course he did. His real name. Except it was escaping him. He looked over their heads at the tents. Several of the other people had moved out into the space between the tents. These looked like older kids, maybe even teenagers, but like these three they had long beards and the same sort of weird outfits. They were watching him and the group of children with the dog.

He realized that she was still waiting when he looked back down. "I—" the name came to him "—was called Carter, before. A long time ago."

Two years ago. Maybe three. Not as long as it seemed.

Nutmeg held out her hand to him. "Come on. You look cold. Come back to the tents with us. You can get warmed up, Carter."

"Howl," he said automatically.

"Okay, H'owl, then."

Hesitantly, he took her hand. Immediately Acorn and Lodge tried grabbing his other hand.

"I've got—"

"No, —"

Nutmeg said, "Run ahead. Take Miss B with you."

Acorn stuck small fingers in his mouth and let out a shrill whistle, even though the dog (*Miss B*) was only a few feet away. She spun around and took off running back toward the tents. Laughing, Acorn and Lodge took up the chase again.

He was glad when Nutmeg simply walked, holding his hand. He didn't have any trouble matching her smaller stride. The people at the tents, the camp, stopped and waited. The one in front was taller than the rest, wearing shades of blue and green, and had a rounded chest and gut. They had their hands on their hips, obviously waiting now that they saw Nutmeg leading Howl to them.

Howl didn't even think of resisting. "Is this some sort of theater? Are you in costume for a play?"

Nutmeg shook her head. "Nope."

He looked down at his guide, her hand swinging his as they walked, her slightly ahead. From this angle it wasn't easy to see her beard or the wrinkles on her face. Except for the pointy ears beneath the long, red, pointed hat, she looked like a girl wearing a costume. *Had to be a costume.* Maybe not for a play, but it was something.

He lifted his gaze and saw the taller, older people waiting, and all of them wearing the same sorts of outfits, beards, and lined faces on all of them. Even the tallest wasn't very tall. Howl wanted to hesitate, to pull back, but his half-frozen feet kept going, carrying him toward the promise of getting warm. Up ahead, Ms. B ran among those waiting, with Acorn and Lodge following close behind. It was clearly a game that they all enjoyed playing.

The closer Nutmeg led him, the more nervous he got. People tended to avoid him these days. It was the odor for some, the worn clothes and ragged appearance for others. They assumed he was on drugs, that he was danger-ous, or mentally ill. People looked right past him, pretending that he didn't ex-ist. No one wanted to face the possi-bility that they could be in the same place—even when they knew that they teetered on that possibility.

Howl slowed his steps, faced with the people waiting. *They were the strange ones, with their costumes and long gray beards.* All of them looked old, even the little kids like Nutmeg.

"Who are you?" Howl said.

Nutmeg glanced back and up at

him. Wrinkles around her eyes deepened. "Nutmeg. Did you forget?"

He shook his head. "No. No, I didn't forget. I mean all of you, who are you?"

"Us."

He let it go. He didn't want to upset her. The sun on the back of his legs felt more like yellow jackets stinging him than fairies now. He'd seen them once, yellow jackets, their yellow and black bodies crowding into the corpse of a small squirrel hit on the road. Like a tiny pack of lions feasting on a carcass, crowding for position, mandibles chew away at the soft insides, hollowing the tiny body out. He had nightmares about giant yellow jackets chewing on him, paralyzed from their stings, unable to scream or move as they chewed out his insides.

"Who is this?" Someone said, a voice that was deep and resonant. One of the deepest voices he'd ever heard.

"H'owl," Nutmeg said, brightly in her high voice, releasing his hand.

Howl lifted his eyes. They'd reached the tents, somehow. The person in front of him was still a good foot shorter, though the bright red pointed cap stuck up higher than Howl's head. Their face was more deeply etched and lined than nutmegs, like the wrinkled bark of an oak tree, gray and weathered, but also vibrantly alive with bright green twinkling eyes. Their beard was thick and full, a cascading fall of wavy hair reaching their waist, braided ends tucked into a thick leather belt. The man—they had to be a man, Howl thought—stuck out a large hand, wearing a fingerless leather glove. Thick fingers, scarred from work.

Howl used his teeth and pulled the mitten off his half-frozen hand, tucked it into a pocket. He wore a thin, worn black glove beneath. A work glove, not a cold-weather glove, but better than nothing. *A gift from Nate.* He peeled back the velcro, awkward with the mitten and glove on his other hand, but he got the glove off. His fingers were puckered and pale like the hand of drowned corpse, cold leaving them numb. The man's hand hadn't wavered, and his expression was kind.

For the first time since—who knew

how long, Howl clasped a hand with someone else. The man's hand was hot against his cold flesh. Despite his smaller size, his hand was bigger than Howl's and it wrapped around his like an electric blanket. Pain and pleasure from the warmth of the firm grip shot up Howl's arm.

"Hel'lo, H'owl," said the man, the same odd accent to his voice that Howl had heard from Nutmeg. "I'm named Little. Let's us git to 'e fire. You look bout froze."

"Little?"

"Yup. Ma's joke, ya see? Her smallest babe, but grew up biggest."

Biggest? Looking around, though, seeing that there were at least a dozen others watching with warm, smiling (*bearded*) faces, Little did look to be the tallest among them. His pointed ears were also large on each side of his head, the tips reaching up far past the brim of his conical hat.

"Good joke," Howl said.

Little chuckled and put a hand on Howl's shoulder. "Nutmeg, dear, git our guest something to break his fast, yeah?"

"Yup, Papa."

Nutmeg darted away, small body twisting easily around those gathered.

"Come on, H'owl. I gut something for that chill."

It was the strangest thing that had happened to Howl, ever, but he wasn't afraid of these people. Hell, he was almost a giant among them, for the first time experiencing what it was like to be the tallest in a group. He followed Little through the crowd. The other people nodded and said hello with soft, welcoming voices. Some patted him on the back or shoulder as he passed. His eyes stung and he blinked several times to clear them.

CHAPTER 6
TENT

It was the largest tent in the gathering that Little led him two, the one at the back, right up next to the retaining wall. Traffic noise sounded like a river nearby from the freeway, but it was both familiar and distant right now. Howl took in the tent, a long rectangular structure in dark grape purple canvas, covered in gold swirls and stars. Above was the brown roof canvas, looking almost like a shingled roof. A section extended out, perpendicular to the roof, a small awning that covered the front of the tent.

Food scents floated on the cold air. He sniffed, and despite his nose being clogged, picked up the rich smell of bacon, and other tantalizing odors.

Little went to the flap of the tent and pulled it back, revealing an interior filled with rich golden light. Warm air wafted out to embrace Howl. The scent of fresh-baked bread sent his stomach growling. His feet and legs moved of their own accord, carrying him through the open flap (*he had to duck his head*) inside. Once in, the high roof meant he could stand erect easily. He stared around, mouth open and warm air filling his lungs, revitalizing him with each breath.

The inside of the tent was sumptuous. Richly colored tapestries hung on the walls, filled with pastoral scenes of people like Nutmeg, Little, and the others in woodlands and meadows, dancing and playing. Several had depictions of tents exactly like the one he stood in now. In many of the detailed, woven images, were other strange people. One showed a moonlit scene with Little's people around a fire with several other taller people, all pale and white, wearing some sort of robes, and stars circled their brows. He moved deeper into the tent, studying the next tapestries. Beside a deep mountain lake, the tents in the same 'V' pattern, was a depiction of Little's people meeting with people more than twice their size, broad, with squarish bodies and what might be fur coats.

It was difficult to look away from these tapestries, but the scents of food drew him on, deeper between the hanging tapestries. The tent stretched on, longer and wider than it had seemed on the outside. Deeper in the tent was a low table surrounded by cushions on which was a feast. Dishes piled with sausages, bacon, bowls of what appeared to be roasted potatoes and carrots, baskets filled with golden rolls, and several glazed pitchers. Other bowls held a selection of fresh fruit. Nutmeg was there, setting down the last of the place settings around the table. She looked up, beard hanging down, and waved at him.

"H'owl, come sit beside me!" She pointed at a place at the center of one side of the rectangular table.

Behind the table, a tent flap was pushed aside and another person came out backwards, taller than Nutmeg, but with the finer features that he was beginning to associate with the women of these strange people. She carried another plater with wedges of cheese. She turned, seeing him and Little standing there watching.

She had to be Nutmeg's mother. The resemblance was there, though this woman's face was rounder and like Little's, more deeply lined. Her beard and hair was paler, almost white. She wore her beard with two long and intricate braids down each side. Here in the tent, neither she or Nutmeg were wearing their tall caps. He saw them, off to one side of the tent, on a sort of rack with several dowels capped with polished spheres of wood.

"Her'e ye are now, L'ttle, keepin' our guest standin and waitin. Come, ye both and sit down, break your fast," she said, putting down the platter with the cheese by shoving a few other dishes aside.

Little patted Howl's shoulder.

"Listen to me Missus, now, H'owl. Make yer self comfortable."

Feeling big and ungainly in this place (*and unclean*) Howl shuffled over to the spot Nutmeg indicated. He removed his backpack, carefully setting the heavy burden down behind his spot, near the side of the tent, where it wouldn't be in the way if anyone had to walk around him. His hips and knees protested getting down on the floor to sit on the cushion. Sitting crosslegged was an impossibility—he hadn't managed to sit that way since he was much younger. And forget kneeling. All it left him was sitting hunched with his knees up in the air, sort of sideways, otherwise he'd never reach anything on the fine silver plate.

Nutmeg sat easily on the cushion to his left, crossing her legs without issue. Little settled himself across from Howl, moving with the same grace and ease as his daughter. His missus took the seat at Howl's right on that side of the table.

It's crazy. Howl looked at his hosts. All looked like wrinkled, old people, with long beards—even Nutmeg and her mother. Except...looking at them together, if he looked past the wrinkles and the beards, Nutmeg was clearly younger. Her wrinkles were finer and less etched. Like the smoother bark of a young tree whereas her parents were more like older oaks. The beards, adjusting to them now, somehow fit their faces. He watched them, waiting even as his stomach clenched and growled from the savory scents of bacon and the golden rolls (*which looked to have bits of sausage and peppers in them*), the potatoes with crispy golden skins, and all of the rest of the dishes. Including eggs, he realized, in a bowl, shelled and hard-boiled. His mouth practically watered. He hadn't had a hard-boiled egg in so many years.

Across the low table, Little said, "H'owl, thank ye for gracing our table." He gestured with his large hands. "Dig on in, as ye please."

"Thank you," Howl said.

He used the large silver spoon in the bowl with the hard boiled eggs and spooned one onto his plate. Everyone else was moving, serving themselves, Little complimenting his missus on the meal. Howl served himself one of the golden rolls, and three strips of bacon.

Then the woman lifted a pitcher and indicated his glass. "Would ye like some juice, H'owl."

"Yes, please, ma'am. I apologize, I didn't get your name?" His cheeks burned at the rough sound of his voice. It'd been a long time since he sat down to eat with a family.

His eyes stung, and he dropped his gaze to his plate. A soft gurgling noise, and golden juice poured into a glass set before his plate. The glass had etched diamond shapes around the base and was thick, solid glass, with tiny imperfections. It was one of the most beautiful things he'd seen. With the juice came a scent like honey and pears, he didn't remember anything quite like it.

She set the pitcher down. "Usually, I'm galled Missus or Mama. Some others call me Mama Root, ye might as well do the same."

"Okay, Mama Root," Howl said. He picked up the glass, inhaled deeply of the scent of the juice. *It smelled like summer.*

He took a sip and it was sweet, but like honey and fruit, not the artificial sweetness of the juices sold in stores. *And a bit like sunshine.* It was as if he could taste the summer-warmed fruit that went into it."

He smiled at Mama Root. "This is wonderful, what is it?"

"Gilden melons," Mama Root said, simply, accepting a bowl of potatoes from her husband and serving herself a generous portion. She offered him the bowl when she finished.

Howl took it, the taste of the gilden melon juice spreading through his body like sunshine, chasing away the cold. He served himself a scoop of the potatoes and passed the bowl on to Nutmeg.

Then he picked up a strip of bacon and took a bite. He closed his eyes in bliss as the crisp, peppery flavor filled his mouth. It was a richer flavor than any bacon he'd had before. He savored the flavor for long seconds before he swallowed. Without taking another bite, he put it down and picked up a hard-boiled egg. It was large, firm, with a bluish tint. It had been sprinkled with a touch of salt and pepper, and when he bit into it, the texture and flavor was beyond his expectations. Better than any egg he'd had, with a rich vibrant orange yolk. He heard Nutmeg chattering with her parents, vaguely aware that she was telling them how she and the other children had found Howl, but his attention was turned entirely to the food.

Carefully, methodically, Howl brought his attention to each item on his plate in turn, taking sips of the gilden melon juice between bites—and each sip required its own moment of reflection.

There's never been a better meal. In all of his life. Nate cooked fabulous dishes, but nothing like this meal. It appeared plain, and tasted anything but, amazing tastes that defied expectations. The rolls were still hot, and the butter he placed in one he split, melted and coated his fingers as he ate. If he had any worry about his manners, a glance around the table showed him that the family was enjoying the meal with equal enthusiasm, each helping themselves to more food, refilling plates, and eating with obvious enjoyment. Though he wouldn't have believed it, Howl reached a point when his glass was drained, his plate empty, and his body lethargic and warm. His nerves sang with fresh contentment. His hips and knees didn't hurt. He realized that at some point he'd actually crossed his legs without noticing. It made him laugh. *It'll hurt later.* Maybe, but right now it felt perfectly normal, as easy as it had been when he was a kid.

Mama Root rose from the table, gathering up dishes, and Nutmeg sprang to her feet to help. Howl braced himself, planning to rise and help, but Mama Root waved a hand at him.

"Shush, now, H'owl. Any un can see ye need rest as much as food."

"Yeah," Little said. "Arrange the cushions as ye like, H'owl. Rest with ease."

It sounded like a really good idea.

He had stayed awake, he remembered, so he wouldn't freeze. Now he was warm, comfortably full for the first time in a long time, his body singing with good food and the kind welcome. The cushion beneath him *was* very comfortable. And there were others around the table, and Nutmeg pushed more within his reach.

"Thank you, thank you," he said.

He pulled them to him, lying down with cushions—*cushions*—beneath him. Softer than his usual rest on hard ground or concrete. A cushion beneath his head, one between his knees, and a final one pulled close. His eyes closed, leaden, and he was gone.

CHAPTER 7

AWAKENING

Sleep tried to hold on but its grip slipped and finally relinquished its grasp on Carter. He blinked against the light. His backpack was beneath his head, which was warm from the sunlight falling on it. He pushed himself up and looked around in surprise.

The tents were gone. He was lying in front of the retaining wall with the sun low to the west on his right. It was early evening and the air held a hint of the cold to come, but clouds had rolled in from the south and were slowly covering the sky in a thick pink blanket. It'd be warmer tonight, with the warm air coming up from the south, and the clouds insulating the earth. Cold, but not as deadly freezing as it had been the last few nights.

Though the tents were gone, he didn't feel hungry. The painful hollow ache was gone for now, and the memory of the meal flooded back. He licked his lips, mustache hairs tickling his tongue.

I need a shave. More than that, a shower, and clean clothes. It'd been too long but right now he felt clearer than he had in a long time. It was early enough to catch a bus downtown and go to the shelter. He could get cleaned up there and hopefully get a bed for the night. After that? He shook his head. It was hard to say. Except he wanted what he had lost, the taste of what he had felt with Nutmeg's family. Nate *might* be willing to help. Getting back together was too much to hope for, but it was possible that Nate would help him get off the street. Even if Nate wouldn't, there were other options. There had to be.

Carter climbed to his feet with more ease than he had expected. Only a slight protest from his left hip, not like the pain he often felt. He scooped up his backpack and immediately felt the increased weight. Brow furrowed, he undid the clothesline that kept the top closed and peered inside. Immediately the fresh scent of baked bread and sausage bathed his face. A bright red, felted cloth in the backpack held several of the meat rolls Mama Root had made, strips of cooked bacon, and several hard-boiled eggs. As he shifted the food, he realized that he recognized the red cloth—it was one of their felted red hats, the long pointed tail folded underneath the food.

Carter threw back his head, not to howl, but in laughter. It was perfect.

ABOUT THE AUTHOR

Ryan M. Williams is a full-time career librarian and a multi-genre writer with over twenty books. He writes across a range of genres including science fiction, fantasy, paranormal, mystery, horror, and romance. He earned a Master of Arts degree in writing popular fiction from Seton Hill University and a Master of Library and Information Science from San Jose University. His short fiction has appeared in Pulphouse Fiction Magazine, On Spec Magazine, and anthologies from Pocket Books and WMG Publishing.

ALSO BY
RYAN M. WILLIAMS

POEVILLE

The POEVILLE series with feline detective
C. Auguste Dupin and his human librarian
Penny Copper might be just the thing.

•The Murders in the Reed Moore Library

•The Task of Auntie Dido

MOREAU SOCIETY

Brock Marsden, a genetically-modified
detective, solves the toughest cases in a this
far future space opera series.

•Dark Matters

•The Gingerbread House

•Past Lives

•Past Dark

DEAD THINGS

Do you like your fantasy dark and
paranormal? Ravyn Washington isn't like
other students. Her grandmother was
called a witch and if the Inquisition

discovers Ravyn's abilities she could burn in the DEAD THINGS series.

- Waking Dead Things

- Dreaming Dead Things

- Killing Dead Things

FILMING DEAD THINGS

Filming the Inquisition at work made Stefan Roland's ground-breaking documentary directing career—calling him the Jane Goodall of Dead Things.

- Farm of the Dead Things

- Mall of the Dead Things

- War of the Dead Things

- Trailer Park of the Dead Things

SCIENCE FICTION STORIES & NOVELS

Discover more science fiction with these books.

- Infestation

- Europan Holiday

- Stowaway to Eternity

- Crunch Bang: The Chrystal Eagle Stories

•Space Monkeys: A Short Science Fiction First Contact Story

•Invasion of the Book Snatchers: A Short Science Fiction Story of Small-Town Terror

ROMANCE BY KATE N. RYAN

And if you like romance and comedy, the books by KATE N. RYAN will tickle your funny bone—and more.

•Watching You Sleep: a laugh out loud romantic comedy

•Tom Scratch: A Short Fantastic Romance Story

9 781946 440976